The Ghost Fish

First published in 2012
by Wayland

Text copyright © Tom Easton 2012
Illustration copyright © Woody Fox 2012

Wayland
338 Euston Road
London NW1 3BH

Wayland Australia
Level 17/207 Kent Street
Sydney, NSW 2000

Series Editor: Louise John
Series design: D. R. ink
Design: Lisa Peacock
Consultant: Shirley Bickler

A CIP catalogue record for this book is available from the British Library.

ISBN 9780750268608

Printed in China

Wayland is a division of Hachette Children's Books,
an Hachette UK company
www.hachette.co.uk

The Ghost Fish

Written by Tom Easton
Illustrated by Woody Fox

WAYLAND

It was a dark night. Sea Force Four had just got back to base after a long day.

Suddenly, the clam phone rang.
"I'll get it," said Luna Lampfish.

But it was too late! Zip Marlin had
already whizzed across and picked
up the phone.

Luna frowned. She never got to do anything.

It was Charles Ray on the phone.
"Come quickly!" he said. "There's a
Ghost Fish! It's scaring everyone on
the reef!"

This was a job for Sea Force Four!
They raced to the reef.

When they got there, it was very dark.

Blob's teeth were chattering.
"What's wrong?" asked Zip.
"Are you cold?"

"I'm s-s-scared," said Blob.
"Stay here and keep your light
shining," Polly said to Luna.

"We'll split up and go and look for
the Ghost Fish."

"Why can't I go, too?" Luna asked, grumpily.

"We need you to stay here and shine your light. Then we can find our way back," Polly said.

Luna was really fed up. "Light this, light that," she grumbled. "That's all you ever want me for!"

Zip, Polly and Blob whizzed off together into the darkness.

Suddenly, Luna saw a white thing
swimming towards her. It was the
Ghost Fish! She turned around, ready
to swim away as fast as she could.

Then she stopped. "Hmm. Now I can show them that I'm more than just a light," she thought.

"Hey!" Luna shouted. "Ghost Fish, over here!"

The Ghost Fish stopped for a moment.

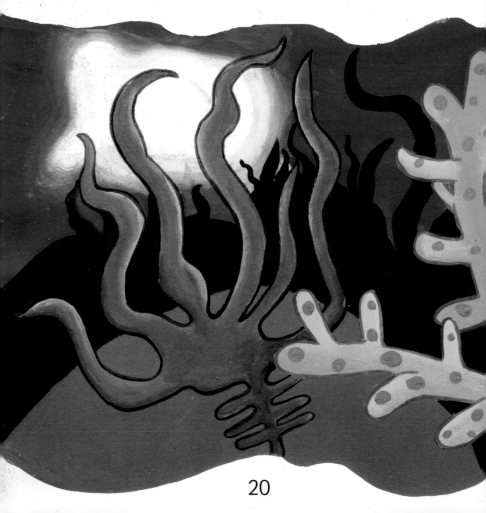

Then it began to swim towards her!
Luna stayed where she was and
took a deep breath.

But, as it came closer, Luna saw it wasn't a Ghost Fish at all.

It was just a big white plastic bag, which must have been dropped into the sea.

It was filled with little fish, who were trapped in the plastic. They looked very frightened.

Luna helped the little fish to escape.

"Thank you!" they cried.

"We've been stuck in there for ages,"
they said. "We tried to get help but
everyone was frightened and swam
away from us!"

The little fish swam off, waving to Luna happily.

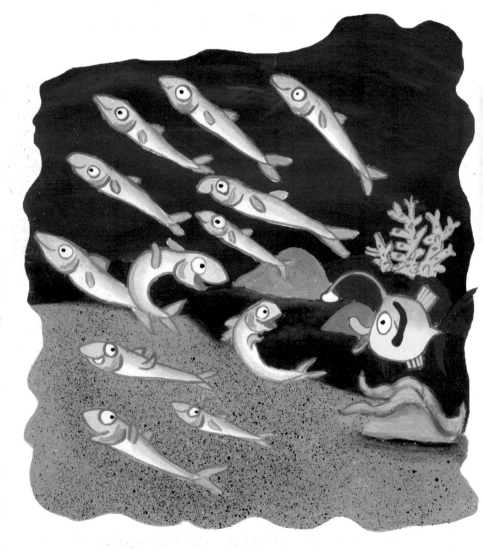

Just then, Polly, Zip and Blob came back. "We couldn't find anything," Polly said, shivering. "It's very dark out there."

They came close to Luna's glow, as she told them what had happened.

"We're so lucky to have you," Polly
said. "You're the bravest member of
Sea Force Four."

"And the brightest!" Blob added.

"So?" asked Zip, scratching his head. "Were the little fish in that bag because they were hiding from the Ghost Fish?"

"Oh, Zip!" sighed Blob, shaking his head. "I'll tell you later!"

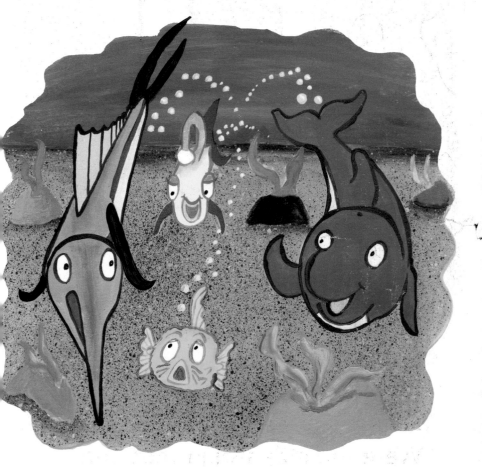

Sea Force Four laughed together as they headed home.

START READING is a series of highly enjoyable books for beginner readers. **The books have been carefully graded to match the Book Bands widely used in schools.** This enables readers to be sure they choose books that match their own reading ability.

Look out for the Band colour on the book in our Start Reading logo.

The Bands are:

Pink Band 1

Red Band 2

Yellow Band 3

Blue Band 4

Green Band 5

Orange Band 6

Turquoise Band 7

Purple Band 8

Gold Band 9

START READING books can be read independently or shared with an adult. They promote the enjoyment of reading through satisfying stories supported by fun illustrations.

Tom Easton is an experienced author of children's books, including lots of funny Start Reading books about the Poor Pirates! He lives with his family in Surrey.

Woody Fox has been illustrating children's books for 18 years! He was born in London, but now lives in a cute thatched cottage in the middle of Devon with his 2 cats. When he's not drawing, he likes to do mosaics, basket weaving and go for long walks!